Copyright © 2006 by NordSüd Verlag AG, Gossau Zürich, Switzerland
English translation copyright © 2006 by North-South Books Inc., New York.

All rights reserved. No part of this book may be reproduced or utilized in
any form or by any means, electronic or mechanical, including photocopying,
recording, or any information storage and retrieval system, without permission
in writing from the publisher.

First published in the United States, Great Britain, Canada, Australia, and
New Zealand in 2006 by North-South Books Inc., an imprint of NordSüd Verlag AG,
Gossau Zürich, Switzerland. Distributed in the United States by
North-South Books Inc., New York.

Library of Congress Cataloging-in-Publication Data is available.
A CIP catalogue record for this book is available from The British Library.

ISBN-13: 978-0-7358-2088-3 / ISBN-10: 0-7358-2088-0 (trade edition)
10 9 8 7 6 5 4 3 2 1

Printed in Belgium

The Old Red Tractor

By Andreas Dierssen
Illustrated by Daniel Sohr
Translated by Marianne Martens

NORTHSOUTH
BOOKS

New York / London

Tony had everything that a young boy could want.
A mother, a father, tons of toys, and a black, white,
and gray rabbit who never came when it was called.

Tony's absolute favorite thing was his red tractor. He called it "Old Red." His father and his uncle Bob had both played with it when they were small.

Now it was Tony's to ride all over the farm, through mother's vegetable garden and along the meadow paths. He'd transport wood, sand, apples, and potatoes in the tractor, and he loved to drive the geese crazy.

"Beep, beep! Move it, guys!" he shouted at the geese.

"Hey, look out!" shouted Ned. Tony had almost crashed into his neighbor Ned.

"Look out yourself," shouted Tony. Then he noticed that Ned was riding a brand-new tractor!

"I just came over to show you my new tractor. How do you like it?" Ned was as proud as he could be. "It has gears, a bucket for digging, and a horn. Does yours have a horn?"

"Uh, no," said Tony quietly.

"Mine does!" Ned laughed. "Want to hear it?" Honking loudly, he looped once around Tony and then rode off on his shiny new tractor. Tony watched him longingly. He wanted a tractor just like that.

"But you already have a tractor," said Mother, when Tony explained that he wanted a new tractor, too.

"But mine is old!" said Tony.

Tony's mother didn't care. "A tractor is a tractor," she said, climbing up the ladder to pick apples.

Tony thought his tractor looked really old and shabby. Riding it wasn't as much fun as it used to be. Not even when he rode it as fast as he could.

Tony was going faster than he ever had before. Suddenly he lost control and crashed right into the swampy ditch by the meadow. He almost started to cry. He was muddy from top to bottom. His arm hurt, and so did his leg. But the tractor was in even worse shape.

Uncle Bob passed him on his tractor. "Tony, are you all right?"

"I'm okay, but my tractor is ruined," said Tony.

Uncle Bob got down and took a look at Tony's tractor. "Hmmmm. That doesn't look good. Looks like a broken axle, I'd say."

Tony nodded. "Looks like Mother and Father will have to buy me a new tractor."

But that's not what Tony's parents thought.

"A new tractor?" said Mother. "That's out of the question."

"Why not?" asked Tony.

"You just got a new bike for your birthday."

"But I need a tractor!"

"Maybe for Christmas," suggested Father.

"But I need one now," moaned Tony.

But his parents couldn't be convinced. Not even when Tony angrily slammed the kitchen door—in fact, especially not after that.

The Herald

Without his tractor, Tony's days were long and boring. So boring that one afternoon, he went to see Uncle Bob.

No one was in the barnyard, but the barn door was open. Inside, Uncle Bob was screwing something onto the motor of his old tractor.

"The oil pump is broken," he explained to Tony, wiping his dirty hands on an old rag. "But we'll fix that in no time. Want to help? Would you please pass me that wrench?"

Tony grabbed the wrench out of the toolbox and passed it to Uncle Bob.

"You wouldn't believe how many times I've fixed this old tractor." Uncle Bob turned and shook the old oil pump trying to get it to budge. "But that's what you have to do when you have an old tractor." Finally, he got the oil pump out and handed it to Tony. "Would you mind tossing this on the junk pile for me?"

"Sure," said Tony.

The junk pile was behind the barn where the cows were kept. Tony had seen Papa put Tony's broken tractor there. It sat there, wedged in among all of the other old junk—used mattresses, leaky washtubs, twisted bikes, and rusty motor parts. Tony looked at his old tractor thoughtfully, and then ran back to the barn.

"Uncle Bob?"

"Yes?"

"Maybe . . ." Tony looked at the floor of the barn. "Do you think that when we're finished fixing your tractor, that maybe we could fix mine?"

"Hmmmm," said Uncle Bob, rubbing his beard. "That sounds like a good idea."

Tony and Uncle Bob drilled, soldered, and hammered all afternoon. They straightened out the rods, built a new rear axle out of some old parts, and smeared the chains with oil. Finally, Tony tightened the rear wheels with the screwdriver.

"Good job," praised Uncle Bob.

"Old Red does look a lot better," said Tony, admiring his tractor.

Uncle Bob nodded. "Like new. You should take it out for a test-drive."

Tony sat gently on his tractor and drove carefully out of the barn. At first he was afraid to go fast, but he soon got over that.

"How's it running?" called Uncle Bob.

"Better than ever!" shouted Tony, his face glowing proudly.

"Glad to hear it." Uncle Bob closed the cover of his tractor. "Since you're here anyway, why don't you take this one for a trial run too?"

"Who, me?" asked Tony, "You mean on the big tractor?"

Uncle Bob smiled. "Come on. I'll help you," he said.

Tony climbed up on Uncle Bob's lap and grabbed the steering wheel in his hands.

"Are you ready?" asked Uncle Bob.

"Let's go," said Tony

"Then let's get going." Uncle Bob turned the motor on. It coughed a couple of times, and slowly, the big tractor started to move. Tony drove it all over the barnyard, past the pigs, past the compost heap, and straight through the middle of the squawking barn chickens.

"Move it, guys!" shouted Tony.

"Move it, move it!" shouted Uncle Bob.

Soon it was time to leave, and Tony rode his tractor all the way home.

In the distance, he saw Ned riding his new tractor. But all of a sudden, he didn't care about Ned's new tractor anymore. He had his old red tractor back. And no matter how old, beat-up, or broken his tractor was, Old Red was the best tractor in the world.